Disney · PIXAR

TOY STORY

Written by Kristen L. Depken

Illustrated by Studio IBOIX and the Disney Storybook Artists

Inspired by the art and character designs created by Pixar

Random House New York

 Published in the United States by Random House Children's Books, a division of Random House, Inc., 1745 Broadway, New York, NY 10019, and in Canada by Random House of Canada Limited, Toronto, in conjunction with Disney Enterprises, Inc. Random House and the colophon are registered trademarks of Random House, Inc.

Library of Congress Control Number: 2009923413

ISBN: 978-0-7364-2640-4

www.randomhouse.com/kids

MANUFACTURED IN CHINA

10 9 8 7 6 5 4 3 2 1

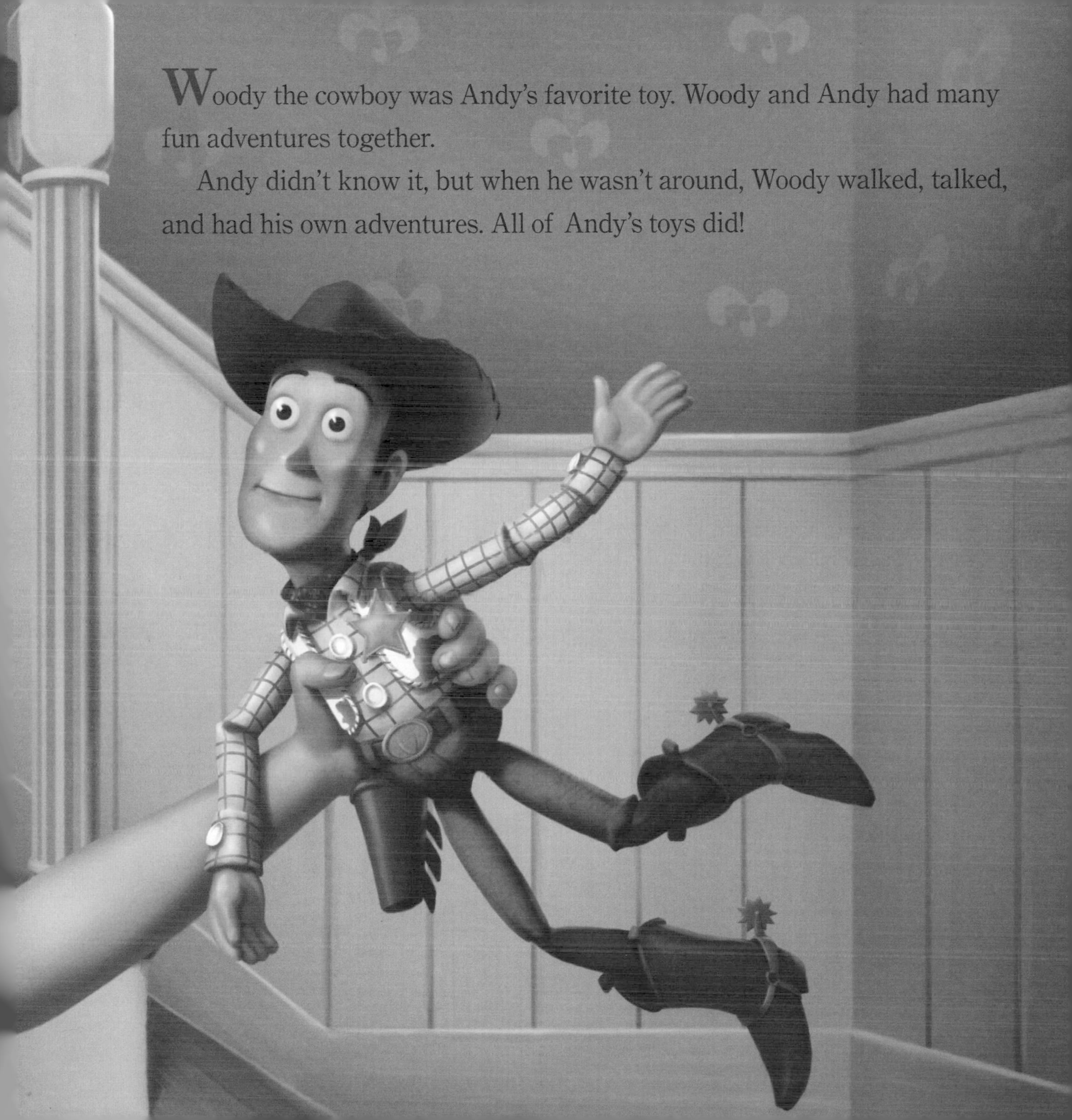

Woody the cowboy was Andy's favorite toy. Woody and Andy had many fun adventures together.

Andy didn't know it, but when he wasn't around, Woody walked, talked, and had his own adventures. All of Andy's toys did!

One day, a brand-new toy arrived in Andy's room.

"I am Buzz Lightyear," he said. Buzz was a space-ranger toy—but he thought he was a *real* space ranger. Buzz had fancy buttons and gadgets. He even had wings! But Woody was not impressed.

Soon Buzz became Andy's favorite toy. That made Woody very sad.

One evening, Andy was going to Pizza Planet with his family. Woody wanted to go, too! He tried to push Buzz behind a desk so that Andy wouldn't be able to find him. But Buzz fell out the window!

"It was an accident!" Woody told the other toys. They didn't believe him.

Woody got to go to Pizza Planet with Andy. Buzz managed to hitch a ride, too. Buzz was angry. He and Woody began to fight, and soon both toys fell out of the car.

"You are delaying my rendezvous with Star Command," Buzz told Woody.

"You are a *toy*!" exclaimed Woody. He was desperate to get back to Andy. Andy's family was moving to a new house in only two days!

But Buzz wouldn't listen.

Woody and Buzz found a new ride to Pizza Planet. Buzz immediately spotted a crane game that looked like a spaceship, and climbed inside. He thought it would take him back to outer space. Woody tried to pull Buzz out of the crane game. Unfortunately, Andy's mean neighbor, Sid, won both toys as prizes!

Sid brought Buzz and Woody home to his scary bedroom, which was filled with mutant toys that he had made. Terrified, Buzz and Woody tried to find a way to escape.

As they searched for a way out, Buzz spotted a TV playing a commercial for Buzz Lightyear toys. He was shocked to discover that Woody was right—he was just a toy after all. Heartbroken, Buzz gave up on trying to escape.

Suddenly, Sid ran into the room and strapped a rocket to Buzz. Sid was going to blow up Buzz the next day!

Woody knew they had to get away. But he had to convince Buzz first.

"Over in that house is a kid who thinks you are the greatest, and it's not because you're a space ranger. It's because you're his toy!" explained Woody.

Finally, Buzz understood: being a toy *was* important. He had to get back to Andy!

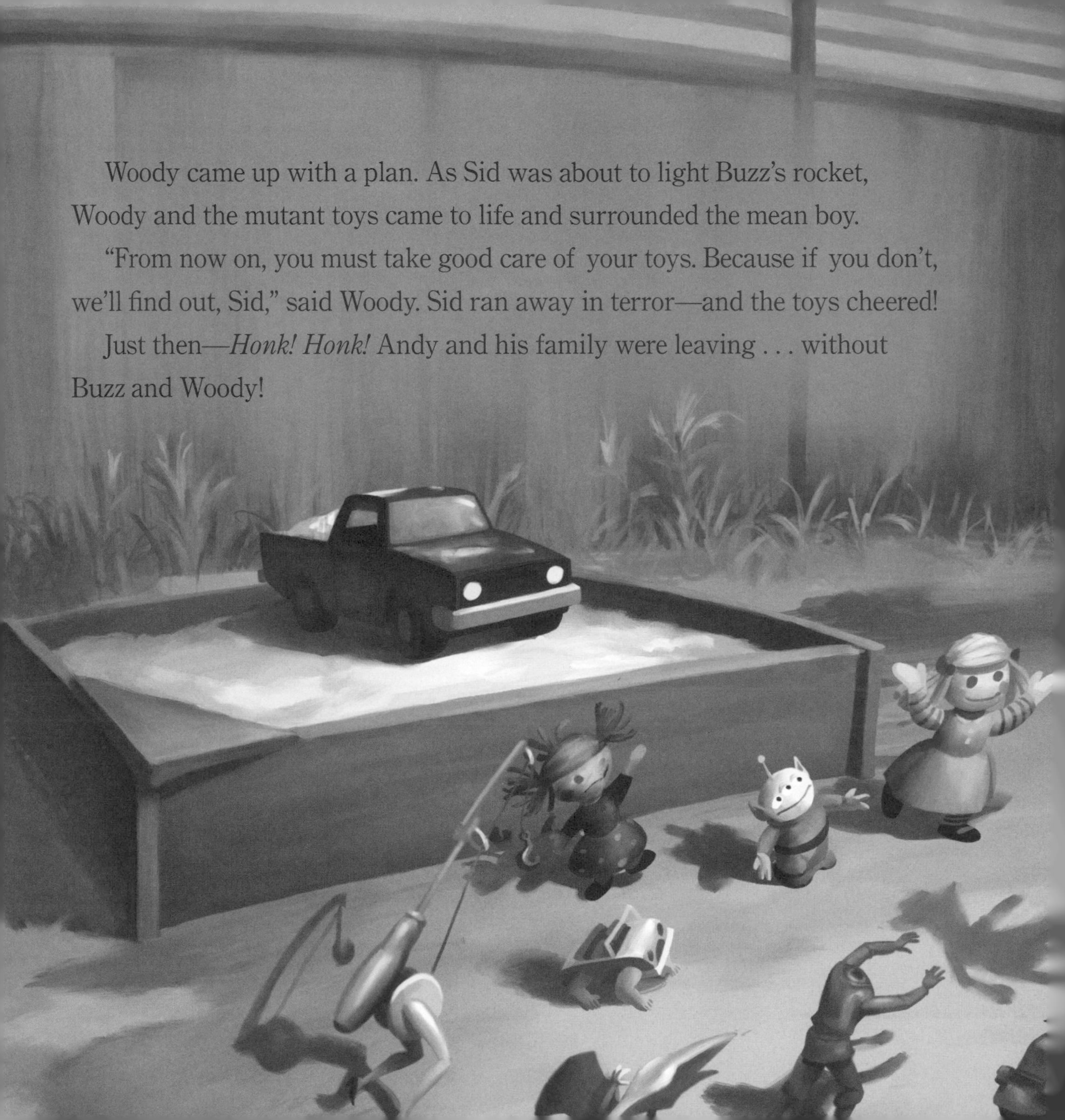

Woody came up with a plan. As Sid was about to light Buzz's rocket, Woody and the mutant toys came to life and surrounded the mean boy.

"From now on, you must take good care of your toys. Because if you don't, we'll find out, Sid," said Woody. Sid ran away in terror—and the toys cheered!

Just then—*Honk! Honk!* Andy and his family were leaving . . . without Buzz and Woody!

Buzz and Woody ran as fast as they could to catch up with Andy's van. Andy's other toys tried to help them. But it was no use.

Suddenly, Buzz remembered the rocket on his back. Woody lit the fuse, and he and Buzz shot upward. Just before the rocket exploded, Buzz opened his wings. The rocket snapped off, and Buzz and Woody went soaring through the air.

"Hey, Buzz!" cried Woody. "You're flying!"

Woody held on tight as Buzz aimed straight for Andy's car.

Buzz and Woody glided through the car's sunroof and landed on the backseat—right next to Andy.

"Woody! Buzz!" Andy exclaimed.

Both toys were glad to be back—right where they belonged.

"Oh, wow!" Andy exclaimed when he got home from Cowboy Camp. "New toys!" Andy and his toys—new and old—couldn't wait to have more adventures together!

Dangling from the plane, Woody bravely used his pull string like a lasso. He took Jessie's hand, and they swung down to the runway, where Buzz and Bullseye were waiting to catch them.

"We did it!" cried Jessie. Everyone was safe!

"Let's go home," said Woody.

Woody rushed after Jessie, and soon they were both trapped on the plane—and it was about to take off! Luckily, Woody spotted a door in the cargo bay.

"Let's go!" he called to Jessie. They climbed down to one of the plane's wheels. Woody slipped! Jessie caught him, but she couldn't hold on for long. . . .

Buzz and Andy's other toys followed the suitcase. But when Buzz opened it, the Prospector popped out and grabbed him!

"Hey! No one does that to my friend!" shouted Woody. Together, he and Buzz trapped the Prospector in a backpack and sent him off for good.

They were happy—until they realized that Jessie had been loaded onto the plane!

Suddenly, Al arrived. He packed Woody and the Roundup gang into a suitcase and headed to the airport. Buzz and the rest of Andy's toys followed them. They watched as the suitcase with Woody inside was loaded onto a conveyor belt.

Woody, Jessie, and Bullseye prepared to leave—but the Prospector blocked their path! He was determined to go to the toy muscum. He had never been out of his box before and wanted to stay in mint condition forever.

"Buzz! Guys! Help!" shouted Woody.

Suddenly, Buzz and his rescue party arrived. But Woody didn't want to leave his new friends.

Disappointed, Buzz and the other toys left. Then Woody had an idea.

"Come with me!" he said to the Roundup gang. "Andy will play with all of us, I know it."

Woody had fun getting to know his new friends.

"Now it's on to the museum!" declared the Prospector. He explained that Al planned to sell the Roundup gang as a complete set to a toy museum in Japan.

"I have to get back to Andy!" exclaimed Woody. But then Jessie told him that Andy would grow up and forget about him one day. Woody began to think that going to the museum might be a good idea after all. . . .

Meanwhile, Al brought Woody to his apartment. There Woody met the Roundup gang—Jessie, Bullseye, and the Prospector. They had all been on a TV show together—and Woody had been the star!

Woody couldn't believe it!

Determined to get Woody back, Buzz Lightyear and the rest of Andy's toys figured out that the man who stole Woody was Al McWhiggin, the owner of Al's Toy Barn.

"That's where I need to go," said Buzz. "Who's with me?" The toys put together a rescue party and set out in search of Woody.

The next day, Andy's mom had a yard sale. A strange man tried to buy Woody.

"Sorry," Andy's mom told the man. "He's not for sale."

But the man wanted Woody . . . so he stole him!

Andy was getting ready to go to Cowboy Camp—and so was Woody, his toy cowboy. Suddenly—*Riiip!* Woody's arm tore. Andy decided to leave Woody behind.

Woody was very upset. "Andy!" he called as Andy's van pulled away.

Written by Kristen L. Depken
Illustrated by Studio IBOIX and the Disney Storybook Artists
Inspired by the art and character designs created by Pixar

Random House New York

 Published in the United States by Random House Children's Books, a division of
Random House, Inc., 1745 Broadway, New York, NY 10019, and in Canada by Random House of Canada Limited, Toronto,
in conjunction with Disney Enterprises, Inc. Random House and the colophon are registered trademarks of Random House, Inc.
Library of Congress Control Number: 2009923413
ISBN: 978-0-7364-2640-4
www.randomhouse.com/kids
MANUFACTURED IN CHINA
10 9 8 7 6 5 4 3 2 1